FIND THE ANIMAL

GOD MADE SOMETHING CLEVER

This duck knows what animal we are looking for. Can you find this duck in the book?

WRITTEN BY PENNY REEVE
ILLUSTRATED BY ROGER DE KLERK

 Published by Christian Focus Publications

Let's go on an adventure. What will we find? It's something that God has made. It's something clever!

Can you find the rabbit?

The Lord is a God who knows.
1 Samuel 2:3

Where are the red flowers?

What is that? It's a nose. How many noses can you see?

This nose sniffs here and there. God made this clever nose for finding things.

Can you find the butterfly?

Those who know God's name will trust in him. Psalm 9:10

Where is the blue bird?

What is this? It's a foot. How many feet can you see?

God has given this clever animal strong feet so that it can dig.

Can you find the baby chicken?

Jesus said, "The Lord knows what you need."
Matthew 6:8

Where is the green hose?

What about this? It's an ear. How many ears can you see?

God made this ear so that it is good for hearing things.

Can you find the mouse?

The Lord knows those who are his.
2 Timothy 2:19

Where is the purple bag?

What is this? It's a tail. How many tails can you see?

God gave this animal a tail to wag when it is happy.

Can you find the sheep?

The Lord knows our thoughts.
Psalm 94:11

Is the boys' hat red or green?

Which animal have we found? It is something clever. It is a dog. Who made it? Our great God!

Can you find the worm?

God knows where you are going.
Job 23:10

Where are the yellow flowers?

A dog is very clever, but God is more clever than that. He is so clever that He knows and made everything.

Can you find the chicken?

Oh Lord, you know me. Psalm 139:1

Is the dog's collar purple or red?

Lord Jesus, thank you that you know me
and love me. You know everything.
Teach me about you and help me to love you.

"Oh Lord, you know me." Psalm 139: 1

WHAT IS THAT?

A shiny black nose and four little padded feet.

Join the animal detectives and find out who it is that is hiding on the farm. He's mischievous, fun and very clever... but not as clever as the God who made him... and you.

Solve the mystery and discover about God who has made everything.

CHRISTIAN FOCUS
Good Books with the Real Message of Hope

J13 CHILDREN'S TEACHING
& GUIDANCE
YCK/ CHD/ PCP

ISBN 1-85792-772-9

9 781857 927726

Places of Health and Amusement

Liverpool's historic parks and gardens

ENGLISH HERITAGE